cl🍀verleaf books™

Holidays and Special Days

Rashad's Ramadan and Eid al-Fitr

Lisa Bullard

illustrated by Holli Conger

M MILLBROOK PRESS · MINNEAPOLIS

To Alex —L.B.
For my mom for always making sure
I had a constant supply of pencils
and crayons —H.C.

The publisher wishes to thank Ramla Bile for serving as a
consultant on this title.

Text and illustrations copyright © 2012 by Lerner Publishing
Group, Inc.

Millbrook Press
A division of Lerner Publishing Group, Inc.
241 First Avenue North
Minneapolis, MN 55401 USA

For reading levels and more information, look up this title at
www.lernerbooks.com.

Main body text set in Slappy Inline 18/28.
Typeface provided by T26.

Library of Congress Cataloging-in-Publication Data

Bullard, Lisa.
    Rashad's Ramadan and Eid al-Fitr / by Lisa Bullard ;
illustrated by Holli Conger.
        p.   cm. — (Cloverleaf books—holidays and special days)
    Includes index.
    ISBN 978–0–7613–5079–8 (lib. bdg. : alk. paper)
    ISBN 978–0–7613–8842–5 (EB pdf)
    1. Ramadan—Juvenile literature. 2. 'Id al-Fitr—Juvenile
literature. I. Conger, Holli. II. Title.
BP186.4.B86 2012
297.3'6—dc23   2011024545

Manufactured in the United States of America
12-51093-10790-6/4/2021

TABLE OF CONTENTS

Chapter One

Where's the Moon?

I look and look at the **night sky**.
Then, finally!

I see it first! It's the Ramadan moon.

Dad says, "Rashad, your smile curves across your face just like that moon."

Ramadan is the ninth month in the calendar used for Muslim holidays. Muslims are people who follow a religion called Islam. Ramadan is the most important month for Muslims. When it is near, they watch the night sky. They look for a new crescent moon.

That moon means **Ramadan** starts tomorrow.
My family celebrates Ramadan because we're **Muslim.**

The calendar for Muslim holidays follows the moon. That means Ramadan starts on a different day every year. Ramadan can happen during any season.

We believe in God, whom we call Allah. Dad says Ramadan is a time to get closer to Allah.

Chapter Two
Thinking about Allah

We get up really early for breakfast. During Ramadan, Mom and Dad **fast** after the sun comes up. That means they don't eat or drink anything.

Muslims believe that Allah wants them to fast for the month of Ramadan. Grown-ups fast between sunrise and sunset. People who are sick do not have to fast. Kids do not have to fast, but some practice. Some children go without eating for part of each day. Some kids fast for certain days of the month.

Today I'll be fasting too. It sure is a long time until the sun sets! Then we can eat again.

On some nights, we go to the **mosque**. That's where we pray and hear people read from the special book.

A man named Muhammad is very important to Islam. Muhammad lived about 1,400 years ago. Muslims believe he was given messages from Allah. Muhammad began receiving these messages during the month of Ramadan. The messages became the Muslim holy book, the Koran.

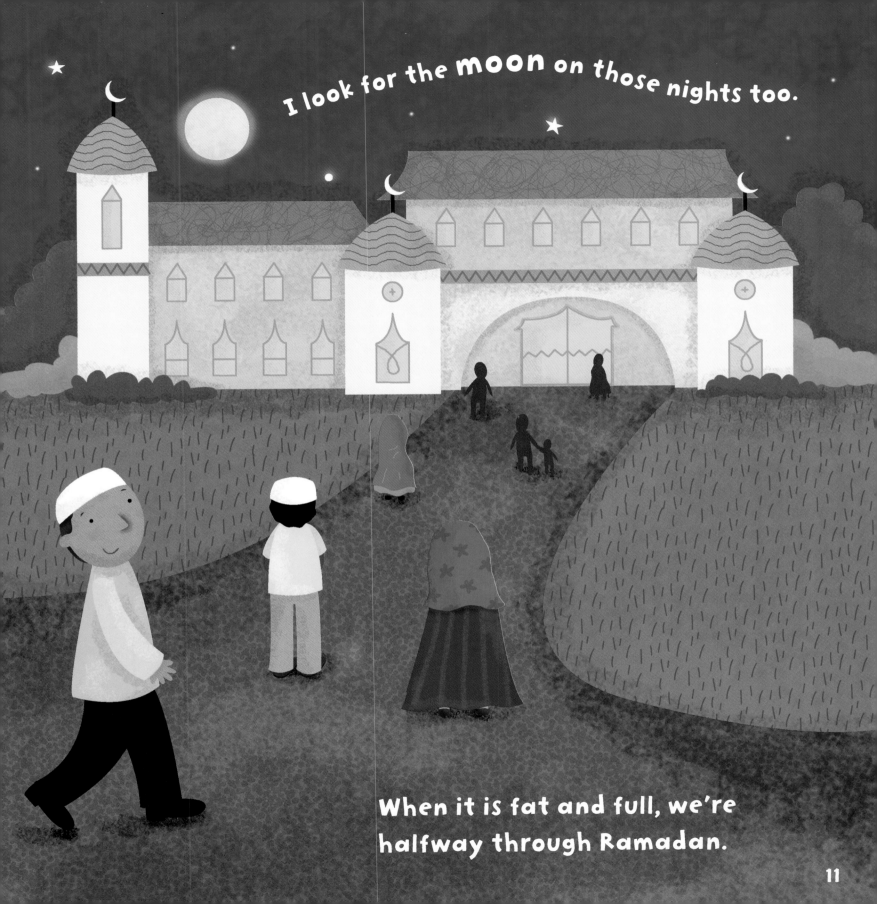

I look for the **moon** on those nights too.

When it is fat and full, we're halfway through Ramadan.

Chapter Three

Thinking about Other People

We all try hard to be good this month.

My sister and I don't even fight. We also give money and food to people who don't have enough.

Helping people in need is important to Muslims. That is one of the reasons that they fast. Fasting helps them understand how people feel when they go hungry.

I've been watching the moon every night. Tonight I look extra hard.

There! It's the new crescent moon again. Ramadan is over.

Tomorrow we'll celebrate Eid al-Fitr!

Muslim families do many things to get ready for Eid al-Fitr. They clean and decorate their homes. They make special treats. They get ready for a big feast.

Chapter Four

A Big Celebration

Early in the morning, I put on new clothes and shoes. We go to a big park with many other people. We all pray together.

Many Muslims cover certain parts of their bodies in public. They dress this way to show respect to Allah.

Dad says Muslims around the world have fun and feast for Eid. Sometimes there are carnival rides and games.

We visit friends and family. People give me candy, presents, and money.

Many Muslims take a day off of school or work for Eid. In some places, the celebration lasts for three whole days. It's a fun time. But it's also a time for giving thanks to Allah.

I've decided. I'm going to watch the moon all year. I know it will grow bigger and smaller many times.

But finally, it will be that special night again. It will be time for another **Ramadan moon.**

Make a Moon Can

Ramadan is a time to think about people who do not have enough. People give food or money to people in need. They do this at the end of Ramadan or before the Eid al-Fitr prayer. They want everyone to be able to celebrate and feast during Eid al-Fitr.

You can share what you have too. Make a moon can, and use it to save money. Then you can donate this money to a food shelf or other group in your community that helps people who need support.

What you will need
an empty can with the top removed (something like a soup can, not a pop can)
dish soap
a sink
masking tape
markers or paint and paintbrushes

How to make your moon can
1) Use the sink and dish soap to wash your can inside and out.

2) Let the can dry completely.

3) Use masking tape to cover the outside of the can.

4) Use a yellow marker or paint to make a crescent moon on your can. It will look like the one in the picture.

5) You can also add some yellow stars around your moon.

6) Color the rest of the can dark blue like the night sky.

GLOSSARY

Allah (AH-lah or ah-LAH): the word for God in the Arabic language. It is the name for God in the religion of Islam and other religions in which Arabic is spoken.

celebrate: to do something to show how special or important a day is

crescent: the moon's shape when it is just a thin curve in the sky

decorate: make something look fancy

Eid al-Fitr (EED uhl-FIT-ur): a celebration after Ramadan is over

fast: to not eat and sometimes to not drink for a period of time

holy: something that is special because it is connected to God or religion

Islam (ihs-LAHM): an Arabic word that means to obey God. It is also the name of the religion of Muslims.

Koran (koor-AHN): the holy book of Islam. It is also called the Qur'an.

mosque (MAHSK): the place where Muslims worship. It is also called a masjid (MASS-jihd).

Muhammad (Mu-HAH-mahd): the man who received the messages from God, which became the Koran. Muslims consider him the last prophet (a person who gets messages from God).

Muslims (MUHS-lihms): people who follow the religion of Islam

Ramadan (rah-mah-DAHN): the ninth month of the Islamic calendar. It is a time for fasting and being close to God.

religion: a set of beliefs in a god or gods

BOOKS

Douglass, Susan L. *Ramadan.* Minneapolis: Carolrhoda Books, 2004.
You can learn many more facts about Ramadan and Eid al-Fitr from this book.

Hall, M. C. *Ramadan.* Vero Beach, FL: Rourke Publishing, 2011.
Learn more about Muslims around the world as they celebrate Ramadan with this book full of pictures.

Mobin-Uddin, Asma. *A Party in Ramadan.* Honesdale, PA: Boyds Mills Press, 2009.
Find out what happens when Leena attends a classmate's birthday party on the day she's practicing fasting for Ramadan.

WEBSITES

The Earth and Beyond: Phases of the Moon
http://www.childrensuniversity.manchester.ac.uk/interactives/science/earthandbeyond/phases.asp
Learn more about why the moon looks different throughout the month. Click through the animation to see how the moon looks to us as it orbits Earth.

Islamic Patterns
http://www.davidmus.dk/en/mest_for_boern/tegneopgave
Click to see the different kinds of patterns you might see inside a mosque. You can download and print these pages for coloring or look at the Islamic art in the museum's collection.

LERNER *e* SOURCE™

Expand learning beyond the printed book. Download free, complementary educational resources for this book from our website, www.lerneresource.com.

My Favorite Day—Eid al-Fitr
http://learnenglishkids.britishcouncil.org/en/short-stories/
my-favourite-day-eid-al-fitr
Listen to why Eid al-Fitr is this girl's favorite day. Then put together the puzzle to set off the firecrackers.